espresso
education

Story Time

Polly's Wobbly Tooth

Sue Graves

D0277403

A story in a familiar setting

Franklin Watts
338 Euston Road
London NW1 3BH

Franklin Watts Australia
Level 17/207 Kent Street
Sydney NSW 2000

Text and illustration © Franklin Watts 2011

The Espresso characters are originated and
designed by Claire Underwood and Pesky Ltd.

The Espresso characters are the property of
Espresso Education Ltd.

All rights reserved.

A CIP catalogue record for this book is
available from the British Library.

ISBN: 978 1 4451 0411 9 (hbk)
ISBN: 978 1 4451 0418 8 (pbk)

Illustrations by Artful Doodlers Ltd.
Art Director: Jonathan Hair
Series Editor: Jackie Hamley
Series Designer: Matthew Lilly

Printed in China

Franklin Watts is a division of
Hachette Children's Books,
an Hachette UK company
www.hachette.co.uk

BRENT LIBRARIES	
91120000201310	
Askews & Holts	24-Sep-2014
	£4.99

Polly had a loose tooth.
It was very wobbly!

She wobbled it
all the time.

She wobbled it at breakfast. Mum got cross. "Don't keep wobbling it, Polly," she said. "It will come out soon."

She wobbled it at school.
Miss Clover got cross.
"Don't keep
wobbling it, Polly,"
she said. "It will
come out when
it's ready!"

9

Polly didn't like her
wobbly tooth.
It was hard
to eat.

It was hard to speak, too!

"I wish my wobbly tooth
would come out!" she said.
Polly was fed up.

Polly went to see Kim.
She showed him her
wobbly tooth.

"Don't keep wobbling it," said Kim. "Try to forget about it."

Polly and Kim took
Scrap for a walk.

Scrap saw a cat.

He ran after it.

"Scrap!" cried Kim. "Stop!"

But Scrap did not stop.

"I can stop him," said Polly. "Look!"
She blew and blew and blew.
She made a lot of noise!

Scrap stopped.
"That was a good way to stop him!" said Kim.
"Yes," laughed Polly.

"But what's that?"
asked Kim.

"It's my wobbly tooth!"
laughed Polly.

"You blew out your tooth!"
said Kim. "Your wobbly tooth
is out at last!"

Puzzles

Which speech bubbles belong to Polly?

Which words describe Polly
at the start of the story and which
describe her at the end?

annoyed

happy

pleased

fed up

irritated

relieved

Answers

Polly's speech bubbles are: 1, 3

At the start of the story, Polly is:
annoyed, fed up, irritated.
At the end of the story, Polly is:
happy, pleased, relieved.

Espresso Connections

This book may be used in conjunction with the Science Area on Espresso to start a discussion on healthy eating and caring for our teeth.

It may also be used to inspire a creative drawing activity. Here are some suggestions.

Healthy Eating and Caring for our Teeth

Visit the Teeth and Eating Collection in Science 2. Roll over Sal's teeth to find out the names given to different teeth.

Open the Activities and choose Multiple choice quiz. Play the quiz asking children to raise their hands for the different multiple choice answers.

Then choose the Word Game and ask the children to choose the correct definitions.

Activity sheets

There are many activity sheets in this area, here are just a couple.

Stay in the Teeth and Eating Collection in Science 2. Open the Things to do arcade. Print copies of the Healthy teeth activity sheet and ask children to fill in the details. They could discuss between them drinks and foods that are bad or kind to their teeth.

Then print copies of the Losing a tooth activity sheet and ask children to draw pictures of what happens when you lose a milk tooth and what happens when you lose an adult tooth. Discuss the difference in losing milk and adult teeth.